A Night to Remember

PRAISE FOR *STORYSHARES*

"One of the brightest innovators and game-changers in the education industry."
– Forbes

"Your success in applying research-validated practices to promote literacy serves as a valuable model for other organizations seeking to create evidence-based literacy programs."

- Library of Congress

"We need powerful social and educational innovation, and Storyshares is breaking new ground. The organization addresses critical problems facing our students and teachers. I am excited about the strategies it brings to the collective work of making sure every student has an equal chance in life."
– Teach For America

"Around the world, this is one of the up-and-coming trailblazers changing the landscape of literacy and education."
- International Literacy Association

"It's the perfect idea. There's really nothing like this. I mean wow, this will be a wonderful experience for young people."   - Andrea Davis Pinkney, Executive Director, Scholastic

"Reading for meaning opens opportunities for a lifetime of learning. Providing emerging readers with engaging texts that are designed to offer both challenges and support for each individual will improve their lives for years to come. Storyshares is a wonderful start."
- David Rose, Co-founder of CAST & UDL

A Night to Remember

Tara Anders

STORYSHARES

Story Share, Inc.
New York. Boston. Philadelphia

Storyshares
Story Share, Inc.
24 N. Bryn Mawr Avenue #340
Bryn Mawr, PA 19010-3304
www.storyshares.org

Inspiring reading with a new kind of book.

Interest Level: High School School
Grade Level Equivalent: 4.3

9798885979191

Book design by Storyshares

Printed in the United States of America

Storyshares Presents

1

"I don't know about this." I watched Finn drop his duffle bag. Things jangled and clanked against each other as they hit the ground. He knelt down beside it and looked up at me with a smirk. His eyes glinted playfully in the light of the streetlamp. I shuddered, not knowing if my discomfort was caused by his look or the chilly nighttime air.

"What's the problem, Aubree?" he asked. "You scared?"

I scoffed. "No, of course not. I'm just . . . unsure."

"Well, you *were* sure this morning when you thought of it."

"I was just joking!"

When I suggested that we sneak into our rival school and steal their mascot before the game tomorrow night, I didn't think he would actually take me up on the offer. It wasn't even an offer, really, just a thought. I couldn't believe we were actually doing it.

Clear Lake and Harbor View High Schools had been rivals for as long as anyone could remember. We weren't really sure why we had such a rivalry. Maybe it was because our names were just different variations of the same thing, or maybe we just needed a rival because there were no other high schools in our county. Whatever the reason, this rivalry had been going on for years with no sign of stopping.

Every winter, when Clear Lake and Harbor View played basketball against each other, something huge always happened. This year, I decided that it was our turn to make something happen, since the seniors of Harbor View last year decided to pose as Clear Lake students for a day and make a mess of our hallways. I brought up the mascot idea, not taking myself seriously at all, and then

Finn got this look in his eye—similar to the one he wore now—and said I was a genius.

Maybe the compliment was the reason I was there now in the freezing cold, watching Finn unzip his duffle bag. I'd had a crush on him since he moved to Clear Lake two years ago, shortly before he became *the* Finn Hamilton, the baseball star of the school.

"Trust me, Bree. This'll be a night to remember," he said.

2

"What have you got in there?" I asked, as the bag clanked under Finn's hands.

"It's my baseball stuff," he answered. He took out a bat with Clear Lake's emblem and mascot (Truman the Fighting Trout . . . how *intimidating*) and tossed it aside.

"It's not baseball season," I pointed out.

He paused and stared at me. "Duh, Sherlock. This is the only duffle bag I had that could possibly fit a lobster costume in it, and even then, you'll probably have to carry the head and claws." The bag now emptied of baseball gear, Finn stood and glanced over me. "Well, maybe we'll have to come back for the claws because they're bigger than you."

I crossed my arms over my chest, suddenly shy of my appearance. "Yeah, well," I didn't really have any comebacks, so I said, "baseball is stupid."

He chuckled and walked toward the dark school. I mentally kicked myself. Fumbling after him, I asked, "Do we even know where they keep the mascot?"

"Well, if I were to guess, it's probably in the locker room. Harbor View is just naïve enough to leave it laying out." He walked through the remarkably unlocked door, seemingly unfazed by the darkness. Once over the threshold of enemy territory, Finn turned to me and held out a pair of gloves. "Here, put these on. We can't be too careful."

I took the gloves from him and regarded them warily before stuffing them in my back pocket. "Finn, we're not in an episode of CSI. We don't need gloves. Do you really think Harbor View will dust for fingerprints?" I didn't really subscribe to the whole "put-down-the-rival-team" trope, but Harbor View wasn't exactly known for turning out brain surgeons.

"Maybe not," Finn agreed with a shrug, "but the Finn-Man does not need to go to jail again."

I paused as he walked on. So he'd heard the rumors being spread about him, but there was something in his tone that suggested he wasn't joking. I opened my mouth to question him further, but he called to me, "Let's go, Bree! The sooner we get in, the sooner we get out."

3

I ran to catch up with him and practically had to keep running to match his long strides. The dude was tall and lanky, almost two of me in height.

I'd never been to Harbor View High before, except for the occasional away games I attended. Even then, I'd never been inside the school. He walked—I jogged—down a hallway illuminated by the street lights a few yards away, shining through the long wall of windows. On the other side were lockers that I supposed were red, Harbor View's colors.

We went through double doors at the end of the hallway and were met with two sets of stairs, one leading up and the other down. Without pausing, Finn went down. I followed with wide eyes. "How do you know where we're going?" I asked.

This time, he did pause, and my heart sped up. He didn't have his normal teasing look, and he didn't meet my eyes when he said, "I used to go here. Right before I came to Clear Lake." Then, he shrugged and continued on.

Man, this was becoming a night of revelations. "So," I whisper-yelled, "you've been to jail, and you used to go to Harbor View? Anything else you'd like to tell me? Do you only have three toes on one foot or something?"

He sighed softly. "Why are you whispering?" His voice was normal, but it echoed off the walls of the winding staircase.

Why *was* I whispering? No one was around. I supposed the "goody two-shoes, never-does-any-wrong" girl in me was terrified of getting caught. It often warred with the people-pleasing side of me. In this case, the people-pleasing side won, as I was now committing theft with Finn.

"You're avoiding my questions!"

He finally stopped at what I assumed was the locker room door, turned around, and gave me that smirk of his. "Your questions hint at a story for another time, doll. Right now, we've got a lobster to steal."

He opened the door and, sure enough, the lobster costume was resting in plain sight, laid out on one of the benches. The parts were all lined up, resembling how they would be assembled on a human body. It almost seemed like a shame to disturb them.

"Why were all the doors unlocked?" I asked, again whispering, as Finn slung his duffle bag off his shoulder. He began to stuff the lobster into it, starting with the body.

"They barely lock anything," he said as he worked. "You going to help me or not?"

Startled into action, I picked up the claws and handed them to him. (He was right—they were bigger than me.)

"Bree," he said, looking from the claws to me with a deadpan expression, "you know these aren't going in the bag. You're going to have to carry them."

I shrugged and then put the claws on my hands because that was the easiest way to carry them both.

"How are we going to fit the head in, then, if the claws won't go in?" I eyed the humongous, grinning lobster head.

Finn picked it up and twirled it around, contemplating for a moment. Then, he abruptly plopped it down on my head.

Forgetting myself, I yelled, "FINN! Why did you just do that?!" I tried to pry the head off, but with the claws covering my hands, it was near impossible. I eventually just gave up and let my arms fall to my sides. "You're the worst," I said with a sigh, even while his laugh echoed in my ears.

"Aw, come on, Bree. You have to admit it's pretty funny. Besides, I'm the only one of us who knows my way around here. Just give me your claw, and I'll get us out of here."

I stuck my claws out for him and gave Finn the lead.

4

He sped us up the steps and out the double doors back into the hallway. We kept going through the hall and out the front doors, past the gates and out into the field, where our mission had started. We came to a stop where we'd left his baseball gear, and I bent over to catch my breath.

I hadn't run that fast or for that long since P.E. our freshman year, a memory I'd rather not relive.

Finn laughed next to me with a sort of maniacal glee. I watched him jump around, hooting and hollering at our victory. Even with my limited vision, it was an entertaining sight. I could almost see his eyes flash under the light of the streetlamp. Then he looked at me, really looked at me, with his smile lighting his face more than the lamps we'd left behind.

It was at that moment that I decided this wasn't a completely bad idea.

It was at that moment that I fell in love with him.

"Okay," I said, finally catching my breath. "What are we going to do with the mascot suit now that we have it?"

"We, my dear Aubree, are going to hang it up on Clear Lake's flagpole."

My brain short-circuited. How were we going to hang a lobster costume from a flagpole? My tilted head must have portrayed my confusion because Finn crowed, "Aubree, Aubree, Aubree! You act like you've never hung anything from a flagpole before. Didn't you go to summer camp as a kid?"

No. No I did not. I'd been far more occupied with fantasy realms in the pages of books as a child, but Finn didn't need to know that. I just shrugged and said, "Maybe I did. Maybe I didn't. That's not important. The important thing is how in the world we're going to keep the whole costume attached. It's not all one piece!"

"Bree, this isn't my first time. I know what I'm doing. Here's the plan: we're going to hang the lobster head on the flagpole. Then, we're going to hide the rest of the pieces in several different locations. I've even left a ransom note in the locker room."

He'd left a ransom note? He must have done that after the lobster head blocked my view.

"Okay, I guess that's a pretty good plan." Even if I was still a little hesitant, I had to admit that he was very creative.

"Well, come on, my Bree. We still have lots of work ahead of us!" He slung the duffel bag across his shoulder and was pulling me towards his car before I could even wrap my head fully around what he said. *His* Bree? Did he mean it? Even with this stupid lobster head? My heart fluttered as I ran, though that could also have been because of the running. His Bree.

5

It was a hassle getting me into the car with the claws and head still attached to me. We had to lean the seat all the way back, and I had to climb in headfirst. The long antennae scraped along the ceiling of the car and were probably going to be permanently bent after this adventure.

I rested my claws in my lap but not before Finn got ahead of himself and slammed one of them in the door. I screamed at him for a good ten minutes after he'd gotten into the car.

Finally, though, we got everything settled and drove.

And drove.

And drove.

It didn't take this long to get to Clear Lake from Harbor View. I had no idea where he was going. I expressed this through a mock-annoyed tone, slightly muffled by the giant lobster head.

I barely heard his chuckle. "We've got a little time, and I didn't say we were going to hide the costume exclusively at school."

That made my previous uneasiness return. "Then where are we going?"

"Oh, you'll see."

I shook my head (or tried to, at least). "I doubt it." I couldn't see much at all through this dark mesh on my head, but I let him drive on.

A few more minutes passed before I felt us slowing down. Then, Finn got out of the car. I waited patiently for my car door to open as well, but I heard the trunk pop instead. What was he—?

My car door finally opened, and he helped me out. There was a pause, and then he started almost giggling to himself.

"What is so funny?" I asked, trying and failing miserably to put my hands on my hips. He laughed harder.

"You have no idea how you look right now," he said. He grabbed my claw and pulled me along behind him.

"Okay, Finn-Man. Where are we?" I asked.

"Your house," he answered casually. "You'll have to be a little quieter, unless you want your yappy dog to wake your parents."

My house?! "What are we going to do here?" I demanded of him. "We can't hide anything—"

"Yes we can because your dad has that shed he doesn't do anything with, so it's the perfect place. Nobody will know it's here."

I'll know it's here, I wanted to say, *and the guilt will wrack me if I don't do something about it.* I couldn't tell him that, of course, because . . . well, I still wanted to seem cool to him, especially after what we had just done.

"How do you even know my dad doesn't do anything with his shed?"

"You said so the other day. I don't remember what we were talking about, but you mentioned it, so I thought it would be the perfect temporary hiding spot. Or permanent, if I can't figure out where else to take the body." I must have been completely still because then Finn said, "Hey, don't worry. It'll be okay. Now, where are the keys?"

"There aren't any keys," I answered, sounding like a robot to my own ears. "My dad never locks the shed."

"Oh, that's perfect! You stay right here then. Don't move." I heard him go a few feet away (he must have already led me to the backyard), and the shed opened with a loud creak. I cringed. There was the clink of the metal buckles on the baseball bag hitting the floor and then the creak again. Then, Finn was back and leading me to his car once again.

"Now," he said, "to the school!"

6

We repeated the awkward process of me trying to get into his car. It would have just been easier to take the head off, but I was enjoying having Finn take care of me. I would wear the head all the time if it meant getting this kind of attention from Finn more often.

The drive from my house to school wasn't a very long one. It could have been cut in half with Finn at the wheel (the dude thought the road is his personal racetrack), but for some reason time seemed to slow for that particular ride.

Then, seemingly out of nowhere, Finn whispered, "I really did go to jail, Aubree."

My head snapped to him, or it tried to, but the lobster head was hindering my mobility. "I thought that was just a rumor," I said just as softly.

"Some rumors are true, you know." He sighed and continued, "I went to Harbor View my freshman and sophomore year, and I got mixed up with the wrong people. We . . . did some stuff and got caught—well, I did. The rest of them made it out. I spent the night in jail but wasn't tried because I was a minor, and no one pressed charges. My parents decided it was a good idea to switch schools, get some new friends, maybe turn my life around." He gave a dry laugh. "That sure worked, didn't it? You know, I'm beginning to think you're a bad influence on me."

Deflecting his feelings with humor. Classic. I didn't know whether to ask what he did. He didn't elaborate. He even hesitated, so maybe that wasn't such a good idea. Instead, I asked, "Why are you doing this?"

The pause was heavy. "Well, it started out as . . . revenge, I guess. Now . . ." He didn't finish.

We arrived at the school sooner than I wanted. Finn shut the car off and got out to help me. "Bree," he said jovially as he helped me out, all thoughts of the previous conversation seemingly gone, "I think this lobster head really suits you. You should wear red more often."

I found myself smiling, even though he couldn't see me.

Instead of immediately taking off toward the flag pole, Finn just stood beside me.

"What is it? Why are we just standing here? We've got a lobster to hang." This was not really a moment that needed much thought. It was better to just do it and think later.

Instead of sprinting to the flagpole as I thought he'd do or even making a sarcastic response in his Finn-like manner, Finn put his hands on the sides of the lobster head and lifted it off my shoulders. It landed on the hard ground with a thud. I thought I saw it bounce out of the corner of my eye, but that was the least of my worries because Finn was staring at me. It reminded me of his look earlier.

Now that I was more aware of my surroundings, I found we were parked under another street light. I could see Finn perfectly now, and his beautiful green eyes that twinkled whenever he thought of something funny or mischievous. They twinkled now, brighter than the streetlamp, and I found myself leaning closer to him, mesmerized.

The corners of his mouth lifted slightly. "I said you looked good in the lobster costume," he whispered, because the moment did not call for loud voices, "but I think you look better without it." And then his hands were cupping my cheeks, and he was kissing me.

I had never kissed anyone before, so I really didn't know what to expect, but with Finn it felt so . . . natural. His lips swept against mine effortlessly. I found my arms circling his waist, and even though I still had the claws on, it felt perfect.

Eventually we broke apart, and he leaned his forehead against mine. He had to bend down, and I was up on my tiptoes.

"Okay," he whispered, "Let's run the head up the flagpole and then put the claws in the basketball hoops. I'll go get the tail out of the trunk. We're going to put that in Mr. Donahue's office."

Oh yeah. The lobster. "Finn," I said, "what just happened?"

"Why, Bree, I believe it was called a kiss, but the French may have another word for it." He bent down to pick up the fallen lobster head. "Come on. Last one to the flag is a rotten lobster!" Then he took off in a sprint.

I laughed. I couldn't help it. I felt the butterflies tickling my stomach at the thought of the kiss, at this whole mission.

A Night to Remember

7

When we reached the flagpole, he turned to me. "My dear, would you like to do the honors?" He passed the head to me.

I took it and stared down at it, glancing occasionally at the ropes going up the pole.

The confusion must have shown on my face because Finn said, "You really don't know how to do this, do you? Let me show you."

He unwrapped the rope from the hook on the pole that was about eye level with me. I watched the muscles in his arms tense and bunch as he pulled the flags down from the top, occasionally grunting with the effort. He took the school flag off the hooks and folded it up, setting it neatly on the ground. "I'm not going to touch the American one. I'm nothing if not patriotic. That's not how you fold a flag, I know, but I don't have time to teach you how to properly do it. Now, the head." I dutifully handed him the head, and he hooked the rope to the chin strap.

As the head slowly advanced to the sky, I couldn't help but think of how thrilling it all felt. Never in my life had I done anything like this before. Not to mention, the head looked pretty majestic at the top of the pole, flying with the American flag, even if it didn't blow in the wind.

Finn let out a yelp and pumped his fist in the air. "Imagine the look on everyone's faces tomorrow when they see Larry hanging from the pole! Now let's go put these claws in the gym." He started to run, but I was way ahead of him.

I could hear him give chase, his footfalls loud behind mine, as we hurried to the gym.

I barreled through the main door and almost hit the opposite wall. Finn was catching up, and I let out a laugh as I led the way. I could feel my heart pounding and my legs burning from my previous lack of exercise, but I couldn't care less. I was having fun.

We made it to the gym, and I stopped in the doorway. It was dark, but luckily there were windows that let in a bit of light. To be honest, the gym looked pretty creepy. Clear Lake at night was colder and less inviting compared to Harbor View, perhaps because of the colors—blue and black versus red and gold.

Finn slowed next to me, breathing heavily but not as out of breath as I was. He grinned at me as I held the claws up. "I'll do one, and you do the other?" I offered.

He nodded and pulled a claw off my hand. We then went to opposite sides of the gym where the hoops were. I watched as he posed at the three-point line and attempted to shoot the claw like a basketball. The claw actually landed perfectly in the net, getting stuck right on the rim so it didn't go all the way through. Based on Finn's reaction—yet another whoop followed by a fist pump—that was supposed to happen. He turned to me and made a gesturing motion, but I stood there helplessly.

I couldn't shoot the claw, and I couldn't throw it and make it in. I clearly didn't think this through. I shrugged.

Finn shook his head, still smiling, and came over to me. Putting his hands on my shoulders, he spun me around so that I faced the hoop. Then he wrapped his arms around me, and positioned me to shoot the claw.

"Okay," he whispered in my ear. My heart hammered in my chest as he did so. "Just bend your knees a little, and act like you're pushing the claw into the hoop." He guided my movements, and the claw flew.

It looked awkward, spinning in the air toward the hoop. It landed on the side of the rim, as though a lobster were actually clutching it.

I let out a triumphant shout that echoed off the gym walls. Finn high-fived me. "That was awesome, Bree! Now, for Donahue."

8

We left the gym, and I felt Finn's hand that wasn't holding the tail snake down and grab mine, lacing our fingers together. Warmth shot up my arm and through the rest of my body, and I fought the urge to giggle.

On the way, offhandedly, Finn asked, "So, do you think there are cameras in our good old principal's office?"

I stopped dead at his words. *Security cameras! Oh no, oh no, oh no.* Our school had security cameras everywhere.

"Bree? Bree, talk to me." Concern filled Finn's face.

"We're going to get caught," I said softly.

Finn shook his head. "No we aren't. I didn't sign the ransom note."

"No! The cameras! They have us on film!"

Finn opened his mouth to argue, but I saw his shoulders slump as reality set in. "Oh . . . yeah. Yeah, they probably do."

"So we're going to jail? We're actually going to jail?"

He didn't answer for a long time, only looked at me with a guilty expression. "Maybe I shouldn't have brought you here."

Something in that sentence hit me harder than the realization of getting caught. He was regretting his decision to bring me on his top secret mission. He'd only brought me because it had been my idea to give credit where credit was due. *Was that all he was regretting? Did he regret kissing me too?*

Finn stepped closer to me and pressed a kiss to my forehead. Okay, maybe he didn't regret the kissing. "I'm not going to let anything happen to you, Aubree," he promised. "Now we can't stay in this hallway all night. We've got to get the tail to Donahue's office. Then, we have to go home and get to sleep. We have a big day tomorrow, that is, if you would like to come to the game with me." His eyes found mine. They were expectant and maybe a bit hopeful. "Would you?"

Would I ever. But he didn't need to know about my intense eagerness. Hoping I was keeping it together well enough, I answered, "I wouldn't want to go with anyone else." However, nothing could keep the dopey smile off my face.

With a wink, Finn grabbed my hand again, and we continued our jaunt to Donahue's office. When we reached the door, Finn let go to reach into his pocket and pull out his gloves. "This time we really do need to wear these," he said. "Donahue will probably think to dust for fingerprints."

A Night to Remember

9

I reached into my back pocket where I'd stuffed the gloves he'd given me at Harbor View. They were light gray and a bit big on me, but they smelled like him, I noticed, as I brought them to my face.

My focus turned to the door, the first locked door we'd encountered all night. "You have a bobby pin?" Finn asked, looking at my head.

"This is so cliché," I said as I fished one out of my hair. "There's no way bobby pins actually open doors."

"Watch and be amazed." Finn opened the pin and straightened it out, then inserted it into the lock and bent it backwards. He looped the other end around, putting that end into the lock as well. He jimmied it a couple times before turning the handle, opening the door with ease.

"Try not to act too impressed," he said, taking the lobster tail out of his duffel bag and entering the room. He stood there for a moment in the center of the room, looking around for the perfect place to put the tail. Then he let out a laugh. "Oh, this is too good."

He took the tail in both hands and fanned it out, picking little pieces of fuzz off of it. He then placed it on a shelf directly behind Donahue's office, in front of a bunch of pictures of his wife and children, positioning it just so that it was the first thing you noticed when you walked in. He stepped back, surveying his handiwork proudly.

We left shortly after that, Finn trailing behind me and actually locking the door behind us.

"How did you get that to lock?" I asked. "I thought picking a lock meant breaking it."

"I can't tell you all my secrets. Some things just have to be left to the imagination. Come on, we've got to go home. I've got a big date tomorrow, and I need to be well-rested."

He took my hand again, and we ran out of the school together.

A Night to Remember

10

Fans were already screaming as soon as Finn and I got to the school the following night. I could feel the butterflies that had taken up full-time residence in my stomach as we paid for our tickets and entered the gym. The game hadn't started yet. It seemed something was holding it up.

The claws were, believe it or not, still in the same places we'd left them. Finn pulled me toward the bleachers. Mr. Donahue was standing in the middle of the court with the two referees and the principal from Harbor View, as well as a very angry-looking Harbor View coach. They were having a rather loud conversation, one that could be partially heard by the laughing Clear Lake and enraged Harbor View fans.

Donahue seemed to be trying to keep the Harbor View coach calm while said coach was gesturing wildly at the claws in the hoops. I could tell Donahue was mad as well, but he looked to be the only one holding it together.

I noticed one of our friends, Selena, standing off to the side of the bleachers. Telling Finn I would be right back, I made my way over to her. She smiled when she saw me. "Aubree! What's up?"

"Lobster claws, apparently," I answered, and she snorted a laugh. "What is happening here?"

"Oh, it's the juiciest thing," she said, her voice dropping lower, as it always did when she had gossip she deemed interesting. Selena was the one to go to for all the Clear Lake gossip. She knew everything and everyone, so I wondered how much she actually knew about what Finn and I did last night. "Someone stole Harbor View's mascot, that huge ugly lobster-thing. They stole it, and here's the best thing: they left a ransom note." She laughed out loud now, sounding strangely like a witch's cackle. "So apparently, the note said that different parts of the suit are in different places. You've found the claws. I don't know why they haven't taken them down already. Anyway, they still have yet to find the body and tail."

"Isn't there a head somewhere?" I asked innocently.

Selena's long nails dug into my arm. "Omigosh, I can't believe I forgot that! Yeah, the head, it's on the flagpole. Someone took down the school's flag, folded it very neatly, laid it on the ground, and put that ugly lobster head up on the flag pole. It's flying right next to the American one. It looks pretty majestic, if you ask me."

I bit my tongue to stifle a laugh. That's exactly what I'd thought. "Thanks, Selena!"

"Any time, girl!"

11

When I made it back to Finn, he was smirking. "Let me guess, Selena knows everything."

"Yes. Well," I amended, "not everything. She just knows the what, not who." I winked at him, and he grinned.

I was still a little worried about the security cameras, but I was also excited. It was the thrill of doing something wrong for once. Yes, it was pretty stupid, but this would go down in Clear Lake history as one of the best pranks before the Harbor View game. And I could say I was a part of it. Of course, I might be saying that from prison.

The janitor was called in to remove the claws from the hoops. It took more time than it should've because the janitor really did not want to do it, but the game was soon under way.

Finn cheered on Clear Lake with the rest of our crowd. His green eyes were twinkling once again with excitement. His fist shot in the air when our team got the ball, and I saw the tendons in his arm jump, reminding me again of last night.

Soon it was halftime, and the players exited the court so the cheerleaders could take it. Just as the cheerleaders were getting into position, the gym doors flew open, and someone came running in. They wore the lobster head, and wrapped around their shoulders was the Clear Lake flag. He or she, whoever it was, ran right onto the basketball court, and chaos erupted. The cheerleaders all froze, mouths agape. The Clear Lake side of the gym all exclaimed with joy, and started chanting the school song. The Harbor View side booed, a mass of voices that sounded like cattle.

Donahue looked ready to explode, and so did the coaches of both teams.

"Finn, what's going on? Who is that?" I asked. "Did you plan this?"

Finn stood there with his usual smirk. "My dear Bree, that would be my best pal Dave."

And sure enough, Donahue yanked the lobster head off of poor Dave Lancaster, who sat with us at lunch sometimes. He now stood in the middle of the court beaming proudly, his brown hair that went down to his shoulders sweaty with the exercise and the heat of the mascot head.

"Did you put him up to this?"

Finn shrugged. "Dave is already in trouble for doing certain other things I don't feel the need to name, so he may or may not have taken it upon himself to take credit for the theft of Larry the Lobster. I honestly did not know he would announce his 'guilt' in such a public, and may I say, hilarious manner." I made a face, and he laughed.

"Why would Dave do this for us? I don't get it." I didn't know Dave very well; he'd always been Finn's friend. Had Finn managed to coerce him into taking the fall for me?

"Let me put it this way. By doing this, Dave gets the credit, and he becomes a legend in Clear Lake history. He will be punished, but Dave could honestly care less."

"I still don't understand. Does he know I–"

"Aubree, last night was the most fun I think I've had in a long, long time. Being with you brings out a side of me that I've never felt before. To be honest, I really like who I am with you. I will admit I did ask him to do this, and it was selfish of me, but he knows nothing about you. I don't want to share this memory with anyone other than you."

I glanced down and tucked a strand of hair behind my ear. "Despite my uneasiness, I'm so glad we did it."

Finn smiled wider and wrapped an arm around my shoulders. "Yeah, me too."

12

On Monday morning, Finn and I walked into school hand-in-hand, officially a couple (we'd decided the day before). Selena stopped me in the hallway, clearly in a tizzy. It seemed that Donahue had found the lobster tail and nearly had a heart attack. He actually made someone else remove it for him because his hands were shaking so badly with rage that he couldn't. Selena said they were going to pull the security footage and see, but they already had Dave.

I looked up worriedly at Finn when she said this, but he remained calm. Later, I heard his name called over the intercom, and I knew they'd caught him. I waited, heart hammering, for them to call my name, but they never did.

I didn't hear from him for the rest of the day. Finally, school ended, and I called Finn on my way home. "Are you okay?"

"Yeah, just chilling at home." I heard a crunch against the microphone. Was he eating potato chips?

"They got the security footage— "

"And they got me, yes. They saw you too, but not well enough to recognize you. And since you're the same size as Dave and basically have the same hair . . ." He trailed off. "But I told you nothing would happen to you. I'm sneaky, you know."

A giggle escaped me before I could catch it. "Yes, I know. So I'm going to assume you're grounded."

"You know what they say about people who assume things," he answered, "but yes, yes I am. My parents 'are very disappointed in you, son. We thought you would make better decisions.'" His voice alternated between deep and high-pitched to imitate his parents. "Technically I'm not supposed to be talking on my phone, but you know me. I'm a rule-breaker."

Ugh, I could just see him doing his trademarked smirk. I wanted to reach through the phone and throttle him . . . or kiss him.

"Oh, well, I'll talk to you later then."

"Okay. Hey, Aubree?"

"Yeah?"

There was a pause, and then he said softly, "We should rob a bank next time." Then he hung up.

By that point, I'd made it to my house. Rolling my eyes, I dropped my stuff in my bedroom and then hightailed it to my dad's shed in the backyard. The squeaky door didn't sound as loud in the daytime. I went all the way to the back and moved the giant blue tarp. There was the great cloth body of Larry the Lobster, sans appendages.

I shook my head as I looked at it, barely stifling another giggle. Yep, Finn was right. That was a night to remember.

A Night to Remember

About The Author

Tara Anders is a recent graduate of UNC Chapel Hill. In addition to writing, she enjoys reading and playing with her two adorable puppies, Maggie and Luna. She wants to extend a huge THANK YOU to everyone who reads her stories.

About The Publisher

Story Shares is a nonprofit focused on supporting the millions of teens and adults who struggle with reading by creating a new shelf in the library specifically for them. The ever-growing collection features content that is compelling and culturally relevant for teens and adults, yet still readable at a range of lower reading levels.

Story Shares generates content by engaging deeply with writers, bringing together a community to create this new kind of book. With more intriguing and approachable stories to choose from, the teens and adults who have fallen behind are improving their skills and beginning to discover the joy of reading. For more information, visit storyshares.org.

Easy to Read. Hard to Put Down.

A Night to Remember

www.ingramcontent.com/pod-product-compliance
Lightning Source LLC
Chambersburg PA
CBHW071225170626
46809CB00005BA/1936